This book belongs to

"1988"

Lauren Rector

From

Aunt Chuggy

ISBN: 002-689080-1

The Nutcracker

Retold by Sarina Simon

Illustrated by Mary Ann Fraser

It was late on Christmas Eve and the empty, snow-covered streets glowed in the light of the moon. In the warm, brightly lit drawing room of the Stahlbaum house, Clara and her brother Fritz played with the presents their godfather, Dr. Drosselmeyer, had made for them. For Fritz, there was a full regiment of toy soldiers. And, for Clara, there was a magnificent wooden nutcracker dressed in a splendid soldier's uniform.

That night, long after the Christmas gifts had been opened and everyone was snugly tucked in bed, Clara crept back downstairs to play with her dear nutcracker. As the hours passed, she grew weary and, too tired to return to her bed, she fell asleep on the floor in front of the toy cupboard.

As the clock ticked away the wee hours of the night, an icy wind blew the windows in the room wide open. Clara, awakened by the noise and the cold air, sat upright and looked around her in fear. An army of mice, squealing and scampering in military formation, marched into the room heading straight toward Clara. At the front of the column was a ferocious seven-headed mouse king wearing seven gold crowns.

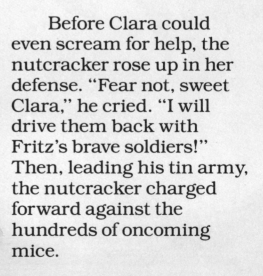

Before Clara could even scream for help, the nutcracker rose up in her defense. "Fear not, sweet Clara," he cried. "I will drive them back with Fritz's brave soldiers!" Then, leading his tin army, the nutcracker charged forward against the hundreds of oncoming mice.

As the battle raged on, Clara realized that her courageous nutcracker was in grave danger as the deadly mouse king rushed toward him. Unable to contain herself any longer, Clara removed her slipper and threw it as hard as she could straight at the snarling, seven-headed king.

Clara's slipper met its target and the mouse-king staggered backward from the blow. Just then, the nutcracker drew his sword, rushed forward, and slew the hideous king.

The nutcracker then knelt in front of Clara and handed her the mouse-king's crowns. At that moment, as Clara gazed into the nutcracker's eyes, she was astonished to realize he was slowly coming to life! No longer was he a stiff wooden soldier; now he was a handsome young prince.

"But you're real!" Clara whispered, "How can that be?"

Taking her hand, the nutcracker told his story. "I was not always a wooden toy. Once I was as you see me now. One day the mouse-king put a terrible curse on me and turned me into a nutcracker.

Clara's heart was filled with sympathy for the handsome young man. "How awful to live with such a dreadful curse," she sighed.

The nutcracker took her hands in his. "But all that is over now; the mouse-king is dead and I am released from the curse. For saving me, Clara, I ask you to be my princess."

As the first slivers of dawn's light shimmered on the sparkling snow, Clara and the prince were swept into the air by a magnificent Snow Queen and thousands of her delicate snowflake fairies.

Their journey took them through Christmas Wood – a forest of dark green firs trimmed with gold and silver fruits and twinkling lights. "Soon," said the prince, "we shall reach my kingdom."

Clara smiled and thought how beautiful the prince's kingdom must be if these were only the woods surrounding it.

At last, Clara and the prince approached the front gates of the castle. The flowers that carpeted their path were rich reds and bright blues – more perfect than any blossoms Clara had ever seen before. And the prince's Marzipan Castle was even more beautiful, with walls of sugar icing and marzipan candy domes.

As Clara and the prince drew closer, a lovely lilting melody could be heard coming from inside.

The music was coming from a huge ballroom where a group of shepherds and hunters danced merrily to welcome the prince and his beautiful princess. Clara and the prince sat down on golden thrones and prepared to enjoy the amazing spectacle.

Dancers from many lands performed for them. There was a Spanish dance, an Arabian dance, and even a Chinese dance. All the dances were wonderful, especially the last one – a Russian Trepak Dance. The brightly costumed dancers twirled and whirled until their feet seemed to fly off the ground.

Clara's favorite dance of all was the dance of the Sugar Plum Fairy. The delicate Fairy ballerina floated across the ballroom as she glided to the sweet music of tiny bells.

After the Fairy's dance ended, Clara and the prince waltzed together through a gentle shower of rose petals and other fragrant blossoms. As Clara lost herself in the music, she felt herself being swept up into the air. Ever so gently, her feet left the ground and the ballroom began to fade away.

The next thing Clara heard was her mother's voice. "Clara, Clara, wake up. It's time for breakfast," she said gently.

Clara rubbed her eyes and looked around. "But the prince and the fairies, where are they? How did I get here?" she asked.

Clara's mother laughed, "You fell asleep last night on the floor and your father carried you to your bed. You must have been dreaming about princes and fairies."

Clara sat up straight. "But it couldn't have been just a dream," she said. Then she noticed the nutcracker sitting on the box beside her bed. Taking it in her hands, Clara smiled. "Maybe it was all just a dream, but sometimes dreams come true."